THICH NHAT HANH

Where IS THE Buddha?

THICH NHAT HANH
Where IS THE Buddha?

ILLUSTRATED BY
NGUYEN QUANG AND KIM LIEN

PLUM BLOSSOM
BOOKS

BERKELEY, CALIFORNIA

Dharamshala

New Delhi

Uruvela
(Bodh Gaya)

INDIA

Kolkata

Mumbai

Chennai

VIETNAM

Ha Noi

Hue

Da Nang

Da Lat

Nha Trang

Ho Chi Minh City

There is a village in northern India called Uruvela. Around two thousand six hundred years ago, a young man named Siddhartha lived near that village. Siddhartha was born as a prince, but he gave up his title and riches to lead a simple life, searching for the path to true peace and happiness. His years of wandering and truth-seeking eventually led him to Uruvela.

Siddhartha is the person who later became known as the Buddha.

The village of Uruvela remains very much the same as it was back then.
There are no big buildings, no supermarkets, no freeways. It is very
pleasant. The children have not changed either. When Siddhartha lived
there, some children from that village became his friends and brought him
food and simple gifts each day.

There is a river that runs near the village. It is where Siddhartha used to bathe. A grass called "kusa grass" still grows on the banks of the river. It is the same kind of grass that one of the children gave Siddhartha to use as a cushion to sit on while he meditated.

On the other side of the river there is a forest. That is where Siddhartha sat in meditation under a tree called the "Bodhi" tree. "Bodhi" means "awakened." It is under that tree that Siddhartha finally found the answers he was seeking.

A Buddha is someone who is awake, someone who is aware of what is going on inside and around them, someone who has love and compassion in their hearts and who is capable of deep understanding. After many years of practice, Siddhartha became a fully awakened being—a Buddha. He is the Buddha that we have accepted as our teacher. He has said that each one of us has a seed of awakening within us and that all of us are future Buddhas.

But this is not
Siddhartha's story.
This is the story of
a young boy who
lived in Vietnam,
not long ago.
His name was Minh.

Minh loved going to the Buddhist temple. He used to go there with his parents on new moon and full moon days to offer flowers, bananas, mangoes, and all kinds of delicious fruit to the Buddha.

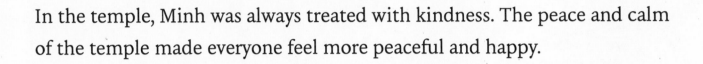

In the temple, Minh was always treated with kindness. The peace and calm of the temple made everyone feel more peaceful and happy.

Minh was also aware that the head monk liked him. He would give Minh a banana or a mango every time he came.

So that's why Minh loved going to the temple.

When Minh was six years old, he asked his father and mother if he could become a monk. One day Minh said, "Mommy, I want to become a monk and live in the temple." His parents thought he wanted to become a monk because he liked to eat bananas.

It's hard to blame him. In Vietnam, there are several kinds of bananas that are *so* good.

Even though he was young, his father and mother decided to let him go to the temple and become a novice. The head monk gave Minh a tiny, brown robe to wear. Dressed so nicely in his new robe, he was very happy to be able to stay at the temple all of the time.

When he first became a monk, Minh believed that the Buddha loved bananas, mangoes, and tangerines because every time people came to the temple, they brought bananas, mangoes, tangerines, and other fruit, and placed them on the altar next to the Buddha.

One evening he waited in the temple until all the visitors had gone home.
He stood very quietly outside the entrance of the Buddha Hall. He checked
to make sure no one else was around.

Then he peered into the Buddha Hall. The Buddha statue was as big as a real person. To Minh, the statue was the Buddha.

Minh imagined that the Buddha sat very still all day long, and when the hall was empty, he reached out for a banana. Minh waited and watched, hoping to see the Buddha take one of the bananas piled next to him.

He waited for a long time, but he did not see the Buddha pick up a banana. He was baffled. He could not understand why the Buddha did not eat any of the bananas that people brought him.

Minh did not dare ask the head monk, because he was afraid that the monk would think he was silly. Actually, we often feel like that. We do not dare ask questions because we are afraid we might be called silly. The same was true for Minh.

And because he didn't dare ask, he was confused. Some people might have asked. But Minh did not ask anyone.

As he grew older, one day it occurred to him that the Buddha statue was not the Buddha. What a revelation! This realization made him so happy.

But then a new question arose. "If the Buddha is not here, then where is he? If the Buddha is not in the temple, in the Buddha's home, then where *is* the Buddha?" Every day he saw people come to the temple and bow to the statue of the Buddha. But where was the Buddha?

Finally, when he was ten, Minh worked up the courage to ask the head monk where the Buddha was. The head monk explained to him that the Buddha is actually not very far away at all.

He told Minh that in fact the Buddha is inside each one of us. Yes, even in you! Buddha is the love and understanding that we each carry in our hearts.

Everyone has the seeds of love, kindness, understanding, and compassion within them. The Buddha was not a god—he was a human being, just like you. You begin as a part-time Buddha and if you cultivate the seeds of love and kindness within, slowly you can become a full-time Buddha. You can become a Buddha whenever you like. When we come back to the present moment and we are peaceful, we can touch the Buddha within us.

The Buddha is available in the here and now, anytime, anywhere.

This made Minh very happy.

Do not imagine that the Buddha is a fancy statue, someone wearing monks' robes or with a halo around their head. The Buddha is inside us and when we are fully present, we can get in touch with the Buddha within.

When you are kind to others, when you love and understand them, that is the Buddha in you. When you can accept others just as they are, regardless of how they look, this is the Buddha in you. And if you do your best to protect the lives of all people, plants and animals, you are being a Buddha.

How to Be a Buddha

MINDFUL BREATHING

One thing the Buddha was very good at was breathing. Everyone can breathe like a Buddha if they practice. Mindful breathing can help us feel happier and more peaceful. We feel calmer after just a few breaths. Breathing mindfully can also help us feel better when we feel sad, hurt, frightened, or angry.

Here is one way to practice: Sit down on the ground like a Buddha, with your legs crossed and your back straight, or lie down and close your eyes. Put your hands on your belly and feel it rise and fall as the air moves in and out through your nostrils. Let your breath be natural and easy—just notice if it is long or short, deep or shallow, fast or slow. While you are following your breathing, you can imagine you are as fresh and beautiful as a flower, as strong and stable as a mountain, or as still as a calm mountain lake.

MINDFUL WALKING

Wherever the Buddha went, he walked in peace. His footsteps were gentle. He was careful not to step on insects or other animals. Walking like this, he felt a lot of joy and happiness. Whenever he felt upset, he would walk mindfully, peacefully. This way his strong emotions calmed down and he soon felt better. Whenever you get really mad and feel like there is a storm raging in you, try not to say or do anything at all. Imagine you are a solid tree in the raging storm. Come down into your trunk where it is stable and breathe into your belly.

When you are ready, you can practice walking mindfully. Just focus on your footsteps. Feel your feet touch the earth. Relax your whole body. Feel your belly go in and out with your breath as you walk. Take a few steps as you breathe in and a few more steps as you breathe out. Count your steps with each breath: one, two, three. Feel the earth under your feet. Is the sun warm on your skin? Can you hear the birds singing? Walk softly, as if you are kissing the Earth with each step. By walking mindfully, you are thanking the Earth for giving you food, air, water, and everything you need to live.

PLUM BLOSSOM BOOKS

Plum Blossom Books, the children's imprint of Parallax Press, publishes books on mindfulness for young people and the grown-ups in their lives.

Parallax Press
2236B Sixth Street
Berkeley, California 94710
parallax.org

Parallax Press is the publishing division of Plum Village Community of Engaged Buddhism, Inc.

This story has been adapted from the story "Who Is the Buddha?" from the book *A Pebble for Your Pocket* (2006). Some details have been changed to simplify the story for younger readers.

Library of Congress Cataloging-in-Publication Data is available
LCCN: 2021035634

1 2 3 4 5 / 26 25 24 23 22 21